Santa Has the Sniffles!

by Diane Stortz
Illustrated by Rocky Katz

Christmas Eve was only two nights away—and Santa Claus was sick! "Say ahhhhh," said the doctor, as he looked down Santa's throat. "Ears hurting? Head throbbing? Eyes watering? Muscles aching?" "Ah-ah-ah-CHOO!" said Santa. "Bless you," said the doctor, and he handed Santa a tissue.

"Santa has the sniffles," the doctor told Mrs. Claus.
"He needs to stay in bed and drink plenty of juice. He should be feeling better in about a week."

"Christmas Eve is only two nights away!" said Santa.

"The children will think I've forgotten Christmas. They will think I've forgotten <u>them</u>! Ah-ah-ah-CHOO!"

"I <u>am</u> sorry," said the doctor.

"But you can't travel around the world in an open sleigh with such a serious case of the sniffles."

Santa closed his eyes to take a nap. Mrs. Claus closed the door to Santa's room and hurried to the elves' workshop.

All the elves stopped working when they saw Mrs. Claus.

"Santa has the sniffles," Mrs. Claus said.

"He won't be able to fly his sleigh on Christmas Eve unless we do something to help him."

The elves thought…and thought…
and thought…until finally one little
elf named Elvin jumped up and
shouted, "I've got it!"
Mrs. Claus and all the elves came
closer to hear Elvin's plan.

On Christmas Eve, the elves knocked on Santa's door. "Come in, dear elves," said Mrs. Claus.

"Dear Santa," said Elvin, "we sent a message to children everywhere that you have the sniffles. We told the children that Christmas will be a little late this year. And look! Instead of letters asking for toys, the children have sent you get-well cards! And we have made you some very special soup."

"Ho! Ho! Ho!" chuckled Santa.
"Ah-CHOO!"
He read all the cards and had a big bowl of soup.
"Thank you, elves," said Santa. "I feel so much better now. In fact, I think I have stopped sneezing. I don't think Christmas will have to be late after all!"

"Hurray!" shouted the elves and Mrs. Claus. The elves filled Santa's sleigh with toys and Christmas packages. Elvin gave each reindeer a carrot and an extra lump of sugar. Mrs. Claus made a steaming jug of hot cocoa and helped Santa into his suit.

Then Santa climbed into his sleigh, and off he flew!

At house after house, Santa filled stockings and piled presents under the tree. He never sneezed once.

But at the very last house on Santa's list, a little dog sleeping on a little boy's bed pricked up his ears. He thought he had heard someone sneeze.